l u o f b g
U F L O G B
Duck
Duck's pond

Duck is snug in his nest.

Duck spots a big crust and grins.

Duck slips and skids.

A sudden crack...

...and Duck is stuck!

Help, help!

Duck's pal, Frog, hops up.
Brrrr!
Ribbit

Frog lends a hand.

Frog grunts. Duck is a bit plump.

Pop!

Duck gets his crust.